High Seas

Doc's Study
At the Sunken ship

Doc's
Lagoon

Island School

N

W E

S

Blue Ocean Bob
Discovers His Purpose

For Joseph

Blue Ocean Bob
Discovers His Purpose

by BROOKS OLBRYS
illustrated by KEVIN KEELE

There once was a boy who lived close to the sea
and daydreamed all day about what he might be.
His island was lush and his life wasn't bad,
but he wasn't content with the things that he had.

Bob said to himself, "I just know there is more.
This cannot be all that my life has in store!
Perhaps if I look for and find the right guide,
my days won't just ebb and flow with the tide."

His guardian, Xena, a blunt hummingbird,

was truly unsettled by what she had heard.

"Just where will you go, Bob? And what will you do?

Imagine the things that might happen to you!"

But Bob's mind was made up and he knew what was best.

So he stepped in his boat and set out on his quest.

"I'll ask the sea creatures if they can advise;

They seem to be generous, happy and wise."

The first one he met was a dolphin named Al,
who lived a full life and was everyone's pal.

"What's your secret?" asked Bob, "You're so joyful and free!

Would you share your success and your knowledge with me?"

The dolphin just smiled. "Why, there's no secret in it!

I simply appreciate life's every minute.

For we are all given incredible power.

You have it right now, every day, every hour."

Young Bob was confused by the dolphin's suggestions.

It seemed that Al's answers just led to more questions.

"Perhaps you should visit my teacher instead,"

Al advised when he saw Bob was scratching his head.

"He's an elderly turtle, and just goes by 'Doc.'

But sometimes we call him the Sage or the Rock."

Xena fluttered her wings and she squawked with dismay.

"I'm not sure we should venture quite so far away."

But Bob thanked the dolphin and headed due east.

He didn't heed Xena's alarms in the least.

He rowed with intent and arrived at the place
where Doc heard the sea creatures pleading their case
for why things should be better or what wasn't fair
or why life was hard and why Doc should care.

Now Doc, in his wisdom, had studied the greats

who had done brilliant things and determined their fates.

He had met with great whites, giant squids, and blue whales,
he had heard all their stories and read all their tales.

So Bob summoned courage and asked the old gent,

"Please tell me how to be truly content?"

Doc tipped his spectacles, gave Bob a glance,

adjusted his shell and rebuckled his pants.

Then he said, "We've just met, but my instincts are sound,

and the answer you seek is quite easily found.

As Al may have told you, you have it within.

Discover your passion, then simply jump in.

Decide what you love, what excites and inspires,

then make that your purpose and watch what transpires."

Bob thought of the fish in the deep ocean blue

And the seabirds and sand crabs and jellyfish too.

As he pictured them all, he could feel his heart swell.

He knew what he loved, and he knew it quite well.

His passion was clear; he just had to pursue it.

Protecting all sea life—he knew he could do it.

"I'll simply devote all my days to the sea.

A marine biologist!" Bob declared. "Yes, that's me!"

"Oh, Doc, you're the best! You're so gracious and wise."

Then Doc spoke some words that took Bob by surprise.

"You are on your way, Bob, that's certainly clear,

but there's something more that I think you should hear.

Your purpose is set, but you're still far from through.

You'll face crooked pathways and challenges too.

So remember for each: Choose your thoughts, close your eyes.

Imagine your wish has come true—visualize!"

Bob took this to heart, shook Doc's flipper and said,

"Thank you kind sir. There's a journey ahead!"

He picked up some clam shells, two oysters, a reed,

and he stuck them on top of his hat with seaweed.

"Come, Xena!" he cried. "I must get on the job!

The sea world awaits me! I'm Blue Ocean Bob!"

Published by Children's Success Unlimited
New York, NY

Design and composition by Greenleaf Book Group and Brooks Olbrys
Cover design by Greenleaf Book Group and Brooks Olbrys
Illustrations by Kevin Keele

Publisher's Cataloging-in-Publication data is available.
Library of Congress Control Number: 2021904200

Print ISBN: 978-1-7363801-0-9
eBook ISBN: 978-1-7363801-1-6

21 22 23 24 25 26 27   10 9 8 7 6 5 4 3 2 1

Second Edition

Printed in Canada

To learn more about
The Adventures of Blue Ocean Bob™
and view other titles in the series,
please visit www.BlueOceanBob.com.

About The Author

Inspired by his young son and with encouragement from best-selling author Bob Proctor, Brooks Olbrys created the Blue Ocean Bob storybook series to share timeless achievement principles with children. A graduate of Stanford University, the Fletcher School of Law and Diplomacy at Tufts, and the University of California, Berkeley School of Law, Brooks is the founder of Children's Success Unlimited. He lives with his wife and son in New York City.

About The Illustrator

From a young age, Kevin Keele has enjoyed creating artwork in many forms: drawing, oil painting, digital painting, even stained glass. His work has been featured in numerous picture books, magazines, board games, and video games. Though he lives far from any coastlines, he has always been fascinated by the ocean and enjoys illustrating its various creatures. He lives in Utah with his wife and three sons.

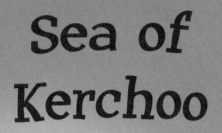

Sea of Kerchoo

Island of Roses

Inn up on High